Game Night

Van Cole

Published by Van Cole, 2022.

GAME NIGHT

First edition. December 25, 2022.

Copyright © 2022 Van Cole.

ISBN: 979-8223437529

Written by Van Cole.

Table of Contents

Game Night
Gay First Time Sports Romance

By: Van Cole

By: Van Cole

Foreword

Danny is an emerging hockey star who is finally setting the world alight after years of toiling in the second string. But with this new role comes more attention, and it will be harder for him to hide his secret from the world, the fact that he is gay.

It's a secret he's kept from all of his teammates and he hates the thought of them finding out the truth. It wouldn't be an issue, if his best friend hadn't returned home and found him again. Danny hasn't seen Matty ever since he left town after graduation. Now he's back, looking for a place to live and Danny is all too happy to offer him a room.

But Danny has always harbored a crush on Matty. Seeing him again makes it clear that this wasn't just a teenage dream. Can Danny keep a hold on his feelings? And what will he do when a rival finds out the truth and threatens to end his career?

Game Night

Chapter 1

It was the end of the third period. I could feel the tension in the air. Thousands of fans were chanting for us, their words mingling in one cacophonous noise. The hockey stick was like a sword in my hand. The puck slid over the smooth ice as though it were a magnet and it was coming straight towards me.

It had been a tough game and I'd been battered all night long. I was barely able to stand and I felt the sweat pooling at the top of my helmet, soaking into my scalp. There was an opening though, the opening I had been waiting for all game. I tensed myself and drove forward, my skates slicing across the surface.

I knew the puck was mine.

"Get it Danny!" I heard Carl shout. I barely looked at him. It was one of those moments where time seemed to stand still. Everything else melted away. It was just me and the puck, and then me and the goal. The roar of the crowd faded into ambient noise and it felt as though I was a million miles away. I saw an opponent coming toward me, I dodged, putting all my weight on my right foot. He went sliding past. I heard his cry of fury and saw the grimace on his face as he went by. I met the puck with my stick, guiding it. The stick was a part of me and now the puck was too.

I slalomed across the ice, my team backed me up, blocking those who would get in my way. Suddenly I was there, one on one with the goalie. Clad in pads, he stood like a guard, his arms flailing, trying to block everything.

All the years of training had led up to this moment. All the time spent on the ice as a kid, as a teenager, as an adult. I had gone through these motions hundreds of thousands of times before, but this was the only one that mattered.

Time slowed. I was aware of my breathing, deep breaths rushing into my lungs. My throat ran dry and I thought back to the first time I took to the ice with my dad, how I kept falling and missing the shot. I thought about all the other times I had crumbled under the pressure and knew that if I did the same here I would blow my chance. A career was short anyway but it could turn on these make or break moments. I could either be a hero or a nobody.

It was as though the only people who existed were myself and the goalie. He was the enemy, standing between me and glory. Then, suddenly, my mind emptied. I remembered my training and all the lessons I had learned. I embraced the void inside of me, the stillness, and felt at one with my body and the stick. All the years of training had turned this action into an instinct. I didn't need to think. I only needed to do.

A smile curled at my lips as I narrowed my eyes and picked my spot. I could almost see in my mind what was going to happen, as though it had been destined. I heard a warning cry. A shadow loomed over me. I drew my stick back and thrashed the puck straight ahead. As soon as I did I felt as though a truck slammed into my back, sending me sprawling to the floor. My helmet clattered on the ground and my stick fell loose. My teeth rattled in my mouth and pain lanced through my body.

But then I heard the klaxon and the huge roar of the crowd. I looked up and saw the goalie kneeling down, looking despondent. The puck had nestled into the back of the net. I was soon being dragged up by the scruff of my neck, my team mates congratulating me. I was barely aware of what had happened, but I was roaring with delight along with them. When my blurred vision cleared I looked around and saw the home fans dancing with delight. The scoreboard showed us up by one and the seconds were counting down. The ref came to us and told us to get on with the game. The opponents were yelling at us to stop time wasting. I was giddy with happiness as I returned to my position.

While time had stood still mere moments ago, the last moments of the game flashed by in an instant. Before I knew it I was being mobbed by teammates again. I'd scored the winning goal and, for one night at least, I was a hero.

They carried me back to the locker room where we all showered and grinned, enjoying the triumph. It had been a long, grueling season and only recently had our form taken an upturn. I was grateful to say that this had coincided with me getting a run of games. Sadly the elder statesman of the team, Billy Rose, had missed out. He was still in the dressing room even though he wasn't playing, and he was the only one who wasn't looking overjoyed.

I tried to ignore him, though, and enjoyed the moment. I was finally playing regularly for my boyhood club. My dreams were coming true and everything was falling into place.

"You have to come out with us tonight. The girls are going to go crazy for you. Trust me, you think scoring that goal was good, wait until tonight and the fans show you how grateful they are," Monty said. I looked at them and tried to hide the embarrassment that glowed on my cheeks.

"I don't know about that," I said, always uneasy whenever they asked me out like this.

"Oh you're not still shy are you?" Liam asked, throwing a towel at me. I walked away from the shower and began to dry myself, trying not to let my gaze linger on any of their naked bodies. It was something I'd had to train myself not to do, because they were all gorgeous, but they were my colleagues and it wouldn't be right.

"It's hard to break the habit of a lifetime, no, come on, I'm just not into that. If I'm going to meet someone I'd rather it be away from the hockey arena, you know? I'd love to meet someone who doesn't know anything about me, who will like me for me, not just because I scored a goal," I said.

The guys just shrugged. "One day you'll regret missing these perks," Liam said. I tried to laugh it off, but it was getting harder and harder to keep my secret. One day the truth would come out. It had to. I was lying to them and to myself, but there was no other way to be. Not yet. I hoped that one day I'd be able to come out and tell them all that I was gay, but until then I had to pretend that I was as straight as all of them.

The coach came in and gave us his post-team talk. I was unable to concentrate on it though because I noticed that Billy was staring at me. I shifted in my chair and tried to ignore his gaze, but it weighed upon me. He had been my role model for a long time, but ever since his injury he barely spoke to me.

"Danny, you did really good out there. Great composure, great technique. You're really coming into your own and it's good to see that all the hard work you've put in on the training ground has paid off," coach said, looking directly at me. I smiled and thanked him, but when he walked away to talk to one of the other players I saw Billy again, staring at me, his features as cold as ice.

I got my stuff ready and welcomed the praise from the rest of my teammates as we began to pack up and get ready to return to our real lives. The adrenaline was beginning to fade and my heart returned to its normal rhythm. The mood in the locker room was always better when we won, and it was something to be cherished, because there would undoubtedly be a loss coming around the corner. That was just the nature of the sport, unless you were a super team, which we were most definitely not.

As I did every time people started to drift away from the locker room I breathed a sigh of relief that once again my secret was kept safe. I tried to hide my lingering glances. I didn't have any feelings for anyone on the team, but sometimes when I was surrounded by hot, soapy, muscular men it was difficult to not take a peek, and there was always the fear that my body would respond the way it was naturally wired without any help from me. I cringed every time I thought about the shame and what would happen if the team found out I was gay.

I gathered my things and rose, intending to walk out and return home. I'd left the locker room and was walking down the corridor when

I heard heavy footsteps behind me. I turned around, and then felt a powerful arm cross my chest and push me against the wall. It was Billy and his eyes were filled with rage.

He'd always been a strong man, and during his injury he'd been doing a lot of gym work, so his biceps were huge. I was pinned against the wall and every breath I took was strained because of the pressure he was placing upon my body.

"What are you doing?" I gurgled, a little panicked about the situation. I glanced around, but it was just the two of us in the corridor.

"I want to know what you're doing," Billy growled.

"What do you mean?"

"Out there, on the ice. What the fuck do you think you're doing? You think that just because I've had to take some time off you can come in and steal my spot? I'm a fucking legend around here. You ain't gonna steal anything from me. As soon as I'm back and ready to play I'm taking back my place and you're going back to the bench."

"I never meant to do anything like that," I said, still struggling with the words as he hadn't relented his grip. "I know you're a legend. It's an honor to be filling in for you."

"Damn straight it is and don't you forget it. The last thing I need is a little runt like you thinking he can take my place. I ain't ready for this all to be over yet, so you just keep your head down and don't think you can make people love you the way they love me," he said, pressing me even more tightly against the wall before he let me go. He gave me a withering stare as he walked away, shaking his head, muttering.

My hand came to my chest and I took a few moments to compose myself, catching my breath. I looked at Billy as he walked away and wondered if I should say something. But that wasn't really the way things were done. Nobody liked a snitch. I just had to not be a pussy and do my talking on the ice, but it hurt. Billy was a legend, and I wanted to be on good terms with him, but he saw me as a rival when I had no intention of being one. I hung my head as I walked away, worried about the future.

If Billy thought I had it out for him there were many ways in which he could make my life difficult. The influence he wielded around the club was massive.

But there was one thing I would never do and that's give anything less than 100% out there on the ice.

I pushed out of the heavy double doors and glanced across to see the baying fans begging for autographs. I wasn't yet famous enough to warrant much attention. Billy was the complete opposite. People were fawning over him. Adults and kids both shared the same look of utter devotion and worship. Desire sparkled in women's eyes. Billy's sexual appetite was well-known, and there were often women lining up, hoping to be the next one to share his bed. Reputation counted for a lot in this world and Billy's reputation was spotless. He smiled, playing the part of the All-American hero. He didn't even look at me as I passed him, acting as though I didn't exist. I shook my head and smiled at a few of the fans as I made my way out, when I heard someone call my name.

It was a little surprising at first, although I figured people might want to get a signature from the man who scored the winning goal, but as I searched the faces of the small crowd I didn't see anyone looking at me. Then I became aware of a hand waving toward me and a smile broke out on my face as I walked toward him.

"Matty?!" I yelled, and my strides quickened to a run.

Chapter 2

I ran across to him and flung my arms around him, embracing him tightly. He chuckled and patted my back.

"That was more of a welcome than I thought I was going to get," he said warmly. I stepped back and took a look at him. He'd filled out over the years. Matty had always been lean, but his shoulders had broadened a little and a dark beard covered the lower half of his face. Thick tawny brown hair came in a curl over his forehead and his blue eyes sparkled brightly. He wore a brown suit, with a white checked shirt that was open at the collar, revealing a bed of thick chest hair. In many ways this man wasn't like the boy I remembered, but the playful look in his eyes was the same.

To my surprise, so was the spark of desire that was inflamed inside me again.

"What the hell are you doing here?" I asked, still astonished that he was standing in front of me. The two of us had been best friends our entire lives until our paths had diverged as we graduated high school. He went off to college, I stayed and pursued a career in hockey. "What's it been, five, six years?"

"About that," Matty said, smiling warmly. "I got back in town and heard you were something of a big thing, so I figured I'd come and check you out."

"And the verdict?"

"I'm impressed, although I'm not surprised. You were always going to be great at this, I'm just happy to see that you're actually doing what you always wanted to do. Hey, are you busy at the moment, or do you have anywhere to be?"

"Not that I can think of, what did you have in mind?"

"Fancy some of Mabel's pie?"

Matty knew I could never resist Mabel's pie.

"Sure thing," I grinned, and we walked over to his car. I usually caught a cab home from the games, since I didn't like driving after I'd played hockey as I wanted to give my body a rest. I glanced back and saw Billy staring at me again. I tried to put thoughts of him out of my mind.

I threw my bag in the back seat of Matty's sleek and shiny car. I let out a low whistle as I checked it out.

"This must have set you back a pretty penny," I said.

"Yeah, a little bit, but it runs well and sometimes you have to treat yourself to the finer things in life," he said. I nodded and then got into the passenger seat, enjoying the touch of leather underneath my hands. He pulled out and we drove across the smooth roads to every high school kid's favorite place, and to the place where we said our last goodbye.

"This is crazy," I said as he drove, "You know, I always intended to check up on you and get together, but it just never happened."

"I know what you mean. Life just gets so busy. I meant to come back here many times but work just always got in the way."

"What is it you do?"

"I'm an accountant, I've started to work privately for a select number of clients. I've managed to fall into a pretty sweet line of work."

"Sounds like it, especially if you can afford something like this."

"Well, you can't be doing too badly for yourself either, the new star of the team?" Matty said, shifting his glance toward me, his eyes sparkling as they always used to do.

"I don't know about that yet," I said, trying not to look too uncomfortable, for I still thought about Billy's threat. "I'm just trying to play well. Maybe in a couple of seasons I'll be an established regular.

"I don't know, the way people were talking about you in the crowd it seems like you've made quite the impression," he said. I enjoyed his praise, and being in his presence like this again made me realize how much I'd missed him.

The two of us had been inseparable as youths and everyone said we were as close as brothers, which was true. Even though we developed different interests during high school we were still the best of friends, but sometimes even the strongest of friendships couldn't survive the turbulent waters of the adult world. I felt guilty for not making more of an effort to keep in touch with him, but I couldn't tell him why. It was just another secret I held within my heart, another part of my shame.

We drove along the freeway a little bit, then turned off onto a slip road. The sign for Mabel's glowed neon against the dark backdrop of the night. It was always open and she was always ready with a piece of pie. If you hadn't tried Mabel's pie then you hadn't lived.

As we pulled into the parking lot I remembered the last time we had been here, when we were younger, different people, and we hadn't even realized our last goodbye.

The summer had been hazy and long. It was the last endless summer we had experienced, as the halcyon days of youth were coming to a dramatic and abrupt end. Every high school graduate had made their plans for the following year and, finally, we were free of the shackles of high school. But it soon dawned on us that the real world was scary, and it wasn't going to wait for us to grow up, to be ready. The following day, Matty was going to leave for college. I'd already decided I was going to stay and I wanted to tell him something, something I thought I'd regret for the rest of my life if I didn't tell him.

The thing is, me and Matty had always been close, but as we grew up, we changed and developed, and I started to realize that I was different. That I had feelings for Matty. I tried to push them away, tried to tell myself that I was just lonely, but the pain bit at my heart and every time we hung out it was tinged with this bittersweet feeling that it could be so much better.

It didn't help that other kids at school teased us for being so close, every time they did Matty rebuffed them, so I had to, as well. The biggest problem I faced was that Matty wasn't gay, but it was killing me, holding all these feelings inside me when they were just bursting to get out. I wanted to tell him, not because I wanted him to fall at my feet and declare that he had been feeling the same way, and not because I wanted him to cancel his plans to go to college and say that he was going to stay with me. I wanted to tell him because I hated keeping this secret from my best friend. We shared everything else. Every detail of our lives belonged to each other, but it felt like I was just a shadow of myself when I was with him because I kept this secret.

So, when we came to Mabel's for our goodbye pie I fully intended to tell him the truth, that I was gay and that I had feelings for him, but the night rolled along, the hours passed. We reminisced and then we said goodbye. The opportunity passed me by and every night since then I've regretted my inability to tell him the truth.

His reappearance in my life may have signaled a second chance, but we had both moved on with our lives. For all I knew he was married, although I hadn't spotted a wedding ring.

The neon sign buzzed above us. Matty pushed open the door and held it open for me.

"I haven't been to this place in forever," Matty said.

"It was a lifetime ago," I replied as I walked in, the smell of sugar and milkshake hitting me instantly. Mabel was there, wiping down the counter. Her once flame-red hair was now tinged with gray and more wrinkles lined her face than I remembered, but she had a timeless quality about her, almost as though she had been a part of this town since its inception, and she would be here long after the rest of us.

The diner was quite busy, as it usually was. It was one of the only places in town where parents weren't afraid to let their kids hang out late at night, because they knew Mabel would keep them in line. But there were a few older people there, and they all turned to face me, applauding me as I walked in.

"Well, well, if it isn't the star of the show, and little Matty Watkins, what the devil are you doing back in town?" Mabel asked, sizing us up with her beady eyes. She placed a hand on her hip and smiled warmly. I nodded to the crowd and smiled as I saw the look of awe in some of the kids' faces, heard the hushed whispers, and remembered how I had been in the same position as them whenever I had seen a player around town. It was the feeling that gods were walking among us.

"What can I get for you?" Mabel asked.

We didn't need to look at the menu. Some things changed, but Mabel's menu always stayed the same. We ordered the same things we always ordered, then took our seats at a booth, waiting for the pie and milkshakes to be brought over to us.

"Looks like you have a few fans," Matty said, tossing a glance at the kids who were still looking at me. "Have you gotten used to it yet?"

"Not a chance. It still feels surreal to me. I've only just broken into the team and I just got lucky tonight."

"Don't sell yourself short, you did really well. I'm not an expert, but it looked like it took a lot of technique and talent to get into that position in the first place. It was a good goal and you played well all night."

"You think?"

"Oh yeah, I couldn't take my eyes off you," Matty said.

I wish that he knew how much those words meant to me. There were so many nights I had spent agonizing about my feelings for him and, in the intervening years I'd assumed that I had grown out of them, but being with him again only proved that they were still as strong as ever and they had merely lain dormant. They had returned with a passion and I was afraid of them.

Chapter 3

"So what are you doing back in town?" I asked as Mabel brought our food over. I had a slice of key lime pie, Matty got his favorite, cherry. I had a banana milkshake and he had chocolate. We each took one bite and made the same satisfied moan. Nobody knew exactly how Mabel made her pies, but she was a magician.

"Now this is the stuff I've been missing. I'm so envious that you get to have this pie whenever you want," Matty said, too preoccupied with the food to answer my question.

"Actually I haven't been here since that night," I said.

"Oh, of course, you have a strict diet and stuff I guess," Matty said. I nodded along in agreement, but the real reason was because this was our place, and it felt wrong to come here by myself. He took another bite, then a sip of his milkshake. The first flush of ecstasy was over and we were able to speak once again, after having sipped the nectar of the gods.

"To answer your question I'm just back for a little trip," Matty said, "I realized I'd been away too long and, well, to be honest, work has been a little stressful recently. I just wanted to come back and recharge, see what's going on down here, spend some time with the folks."

"How long are you staying for?" I asked, trying not to sound too hopeful. If it was just a trip like this then he was probably only staying for a few nights at most. That didn't seem like much time at all.

"I'm undecided yet. I have a little gap in my schedule and a lot of the work I can do from anywhere I like so I'm not in a rush to get back. I just wanted to take some time for myself."

"You staying at your folks?"

"I thought about it but I went there for dinner and realized that I couldn't handle going back there, not for more than a few nights. I'll probably get a hotel room. It won't be homey but it'll do."

"Don't worry about that, come and crash at mine."

"You sure?"

"Yeah, I've got plenty of room, and it'll be good to have someone else around. It'll give us a chance to catch up properly. Besides, we always did say we wanted to live together one day."

"Yeah, we did, didn't we? We said a lot of things though," Matty said, a wistful tint to his voice.

"We did, I guess a lot of them were just stupid childish dreams."

"Some were but not all of them. You're living the dream," Matty said.

"So are you it looks like, you're probably the most successful person to leave this place in a long time."

"Maybe," Matty said, then looked around at the diner. "Damn, do you remember the last time we were here?"

"How can I forget? Our last night together."

"I can't believe how much has changed since then. I was so scared to go off to college. Even at the last minute I was tempted to just pack it all in and stay here."

"I bet you're glad you didn't though."

"Hell yeah."

"So what's life been like? Was college crazy? You dating anyone?"

"It's been good, yes, it was, although not as crazy as you'd expect and, no, I'm not dating anyone right now. I was for a little while but it didn't work out. I thought it was going to be one of those special things for a while but eventually we realized we weren't right for each other."

"Oh, I'm sorry to hear that," I said, although secretly I was jealous that he'd shared his heart with someone.

"What about you? You must be drowning in girls."

"I think you have a bit of a misconception about what it's like to be a hockey player," I said, smiling in amusement. "To be honest with you I don't really have the time. I spend most of it training, and when I'm not training I'm studying videos and things, to try and get any edge in my performance," I said, trying to make the lie sound legitimate. In truth, I wasn't entirely sure why I was so afraid of telling Matty the truth. If there was anyone who would understand, it was him. I think that I had kept the secret for so long it had just become habit.

"When you put it like that we both sound like losers. Remember when we said that we'd have gorgeous wives to rub in the faces of all the girls who rejected us at school?" Matty asked.

"I remember."

"Damn, time goes by too quickly. I always thought I'd be further ahead than I am at this point."

"I'm sure there are other people who feel the same. You can look at anyone and think that you're not doing so well as them in some respects, what really matters is that you're happy. Are you happy, Matty?"

Matty shrugged and said that he was. If we had just been mere acquaintances, I probably would have accepted his answer and carried on with the conversation, but I knew him better than anyone even though we hadn't spoken in years.

"You want to talk about it?"

"Not right now Danny, I just want to think about the good times, when we were younger and we didn't have anything to worry about," he said, smiling. So that's what we did. We spent the rest of the night sharing memories about all the trouble we used to get into, talking about what had happened to other members of our graduating class, resurrecting old jokes that nobody except us would find funny, as we fell into a comfortable and familiar routine. It was as though we had not actually been apart for all those years, as though we had never said goodbye.

Chapter 4

We stayed at Mabel's until closing. I felt guilty for having had two slices of pie and two milkshakes, but I told myself I'd work it off in training and that I was allowed a little indulgence now and then. We walked back to Matty's car and then returned to my apartment. The roads were practically empty at this time of night so it was a short drive and I just hoped it wasn't too messy for him.

He was impressed with the location. My apartment looked over the bay. When we got inside, I began to pick up a few things that had been left strewn around, while he went to the balcony and stared out at the bay. I joined him a few moments later.

The air was warm and smelled of summer. The water in the bay was still, as though an inky black cloak had been laid across the world. A few boats were in the bay and glittering pinpricks of light were dotted around the shore. Matty had both hands on the edge of the balcony and inhaled deeply.

"You are a lucky man. I'd love to have a view like this, just somewhere I could come to look out at a peaceful scene and forget about everything," Matty said.

The moon hung high in the sky and we stood there in silent reverence. I tried not to stare at him, for the more I looked at him the more attractive I found him. My gut tightened and twisted. I wanted to tell him so many things. It would be so easy, I told myself, just to let the words spill out, but I couldn't bring myself to begin.

"I've missed you a lot Danny. I often wonder what our lives would have been like if things had worked out differently, if I'd have stayed here, or if you'd come to college with me," Matty said.

"I think the same thing. I guess we can't fight against life though."

"No, I guess we can't," he said mournfully. We spent a few more moments on the balcony before he said he was going to turn in for the night. I showed him where everything was, then left him in the guest room while I went in the lounge to have some water before bed. I reflected on the time we spent together. Something definitely seemed amiss with him. Matty was never the spontaneous type, so for him to show up out of the blue like this was surprising, and it made me wonder what was really going on. Perhaps it was just the lingering heartbreak over the relationship he mentioned, but I would support him, and I'd be there for him as long as he needed it, and if the opportunity presented itself I'd tell him how I felt. It was time I started to relieve myself of the burdens that I had been carrying for so long, as long as I wouldn't merely be passing my burdens on to Matty.

I went to bed thinking back to the boy I used to be, the one who was partners in crime with Matty. I relived the memories we shared and wondered, indeed, what life would have been like had I told him how I felt. Even though Matty wasn't gay I wondered if he had any kind of subtle feeling for me. Perhaps, if I had told him, he would have been willing to open his heart to the possibility.

More likely, it would have changed things irrevocably. Maybe it was for the best that I didn't let our friendship end on a sour note. It wasn't as though he could have changed his plans and stayed here. It was too sudden, too abrupt, too much like something out of a movie, when we all know that things in real life are far more complex and muddy. I'd looked up stories about people who revealed long-held feelings for friends, as well, and very few of them had happy endings. Mostly, they ended up losing the connection that was so special, and part of me wondered if I should even risk it. But, then, I decided that since Matty and I hadn't spoken in years, there wasn't really much to jeopardize.

Chapter 5

My sleep was restless and when I awoke in the morning I got straight out of bed, not wanting to waste the day. The sun had risen and was glowing over the bay, casting it in a golden light. Some people were already taking their boats out, making the most of the beautiful weather. I had a contented feeling within my heart and was looking forward to spending more time with Matty. Even if I didn't tell him about my feelings I still wanted to enjoy the time we spent together, for however long it lasted.

I did my morning exercises and then had breakfast. It was at this point that Matty woke up and stumbled out of bed. He never had been a morning person. His hair was unkempt and he wore no top. He yawned as he greeted me, but woke up when he saw the box of cereal.

"I was just going to watch last night's game, if you don't mind?" I asked. Matty shook his head and told me to carry on. I perched myself in front of the television with my notepad and started the game. Matty joined me, curling his legs underneath him, crunching on his cereal.

"Do you all have to do this?" Matty asked.

"Not all of us, but it's encouraged. I think a lot of the younger ones do it automatically because we're more used to the idea of analyzing our performances like this. Some of the older players don't bother."

"I guess there's a lot more to the job than just playing hockey."

"Oh, yeah, I train a lot and when I'm not training, I'm watching other games, looking at other players to see if there's anything I can adjust for the next game. I look at the opponents coming up to see if there are any weaknesses to exploit."

"You always were a good student, deep down you're just a geek aren't you," Matty teased.

"Maybe," I grinned, and turned my attention back to the game. I ended up with about a page and a half of notes, but I stopped writing when it was my moment of glory. "Sometimes it's hard to believe that I'm watching myself on the screen," I admitted.

"It must be pretty surreal. Think you'll ever get a trading card or something?" Matty asked.

"If they do, I hope they get a better picture than my current roster photo," I joked. I turned off the match and then stretched a little and took the bowls back to the sink. I began to wash up, but Matty leapt up and said that he would do it. I told him it wasn't necessary.

"I insist," Matty said, "you've shown me hospitality and I'm not going to be one of those people who just take, take, take. And I'm going to pay you something towards rent as well, and don't even try telling me that it's not necessary. I'm not going to mooch off you," he said. I raised my eyebrows and held up my hands in surrender. Matty was always forthright about this stuff and I knew I wouldn't be able to talk him out of it.

"What are you going to do today?" I asked.

"That kinda depends on you. Are you going into training today?"

"I'll probably go for a run, but we always get the day after a game off," I said.

"You want to hang out later?"

"Well, you could always come for a run with me, of course," I said. Matty laughed and slapped his belly, telling me that he wasn't in much of a shape to run. I shook my head and told him that I'd love to do something. I waited a little while for my breakfast to settle before I went for a run around the bay, breathing in the smells of the water and enjoying the sight of the endless horizon. Just having Matty back made me feel better. Life had been good to me and I had accomplished a lot in his absence, but it somehow seemed less special than it would have been if Matty had been with me through it all.

I knew he was only here for a short time but I wasn't ready to think about the prospect of him leaving yet.

When I returned from my run there was no sign of Matty. I figured he had popped out to see his parents or another old friend, so I jumped in the shower and enjoyed the warm soapy water cascading down my body. I lathered myself well and looked forward to spending the day with Matty, wondering what he had in mind for us to do together.

When I was finished I wrapped a towel around my waist and left the bathroom, only to collide with Matty on my exit. The shock was such that I jumped back and the towel loosened from around my waist and it fell to the floor. There was a moment of shock and horror as we both looked down at my naked body. Then my hands fell to my crotch in an effort to be modest.

Matty just laughed.

I picked up the towel and wrapped it around my waist again.

"I didn't mean to make you jump," Matty said. My cheeks flushed crimson with embarrassment and I tried to stammer out an apology but he told me not to worry. I retreated to my room, cringing the entire way, feeling so stupid for letting it happen and for wishing that he hadn't laughed but had instead reached out an eager hand to explore my body. Tension rose within me. Because of my situation I hadn't been laid in a long time, not since a trip out of state a year or so ago and I was just about ready to burst. The thought of someone else seeing me naked thrilled me, I only wished that it had led to something more.

It took me about an hour before I summoned enough courage to leave my room and venture outside to face Matty again. When I did so, I wore a sheepish look.

"I'm so sorry for what happened earlier," I said.

"Don't worry about it. We've been friends long enough that it's no big deal. There's not really much we haven't shared with each other, is there?" he asked. It was almost like a challenge, daring me to tell him the truth. "Anyway, let's go, I've got a good day planned," he said, grabbing a jacket and throwing it at me.

Chapter 6

I had no idea where Matty was taking me but we ended up at a mini golf course. The small windmills rotated slowly and I remembered the competitions we'd had here when we were younger.

"Think you can beat me now?" I asked.

"I'm going to give it my best shot. For all you know that's what I've been doing over the years, practicing my mini golf skills."

"If you have then it was time wasted my friend because you'll never beat me," I said, smiling at the thought of how many competitive events I had won against him over the years. I'd always had a natural affinity for sports, while he had developed a gift for numbers. But one thing I loved about Matty was that he was always a good sport. Whenever he lost he took it with grace and good humor, and he always put up a good fight.

The same was true now, although, despite his claims, he evidently hadn't been spending time developing his mini golf skills because he was just as terrible as he ever was, but it was all in good fun.

We laughed and joked, and although I didn't want to think about our dynamic it did feel like this was what a date should be like. We were on the same wavelength, finishing each others' sentences. I supposed when he came back there was a little part of me that wondered if things had changed and that I'd realize my feelings for him had been the product of my confusion as a youth. The more time I spent with him the more I realized that my feelings were stronger than they had ever been.

The way he laughed sparked a harmony in my mind, whenever he was close to me, my body bristled with tension. I gazed at his lips when I thought he wasn't looking and longed to have them kissing me, touching me. I thought back to all the conversations we had shared, all the secrets we'd exchanged. I thought about how he made me feel like a better person, like I could do anything. My heart beat for him, fiercely and strongly, but it was imprisoned, beating only for itself, unable to share the love that wanted to burst out with the strength of a supernova.

After golf we went for lunch, and then for a walk along the bay. We ended up sitting next to each other on a hill, away from the rest of the world. It was peaceful, still, and it felt as though the only thing that mattered to us was each other. There was a burning question on my mind though, one that I thought I needed an answer to.

"Why did you really come back Matty? I know there's something on your mind, and it's not like you just to take a trip randomly," I said.

"Maybe I've changed over the years."

"Maybe in some ways, but not in the ways that matter. You can tell me anything, you know, I won't judge you."

Matty grinned and sighed, looking out to the water. "I never was able to hide anything from you," he said. He reached down and picked up some grass, tearing it between his fingers, something he had always done when he was nervous. "You ever get into a situation and it suddenly becomes so big that you can't control it? Like the world is just spiraling around you and you're trying to reach out and grasp something to steady yourself but there's nothing to hold onto?"

"I'm not sure I understand. I don't think I've ever had anything like that but I want you to tell me what's going on. I want to help," I said, looking toward him with concern. The way he spoke troubled me, as did the way he suddenly looked so haggard, as though he had aged twenty years in an instant. His eyes looked haunted.

He looked around us, as if to ensure that nobody was listening. The carefree days of our youth were behind us. I suddenly felt guilty for not being there for Matty through the years, for not picking up the phone to give him a call or making the effort to go and see him. I had been so consumed by my own feelings for him, so ashamed at the thought of indulging them, that I had neglected him as a friend.

"You remember I told you that I work privately for a few different clients?" he began, each word as sharp as ice. "Well, some of them aren't as reputable as I'd hoped. I didn't realize it at first. I thought they were just businessmen and entrepreneurs, but when I started to look at the accounts I realized that something was very, very wrong, and now I don't know what to do. These people, they're dangerous, you know? I've already received a couple of threats after I raised concerns. What they're doing is illegal and if it's discovered that I'm their accountant I could get in serious trouble, but if I go to the police and they find out I could be hurt, or worse. That's why I wanted to come back here. I told them that I had a family emergency but I can't stave them off for long. I'm going to need to go back to them soon and tell them something. I shouldn't be messed up with this. I should have just done my time in a normal firm but I was stupid and greedy. I wanted everything quicker than it was coming and when I saw an opportunity that seemed too good to be true I took it without thinking. I'm such an idiot," he said, hanging his head, sighing loudly.

I put my hand on his back, offering him support without trying to be too intimate.

"I'm sure you'll figure something out and you always have a place here. I've got your back. Anything you need I'll give you," I said.

"Thanks Danny, I owe you," he said, his eyes tinged with sadness. I looked at my friend and saw how the world had shaken him, how he had returned to the warm bosom of home for some comfort, and knew that I had to try and help him.

"Come on," I said, pulling him up. He asked me where we were going. I told him that he wasn't allowed to be sad today. We went to the cinema and saw a movie. We shared some popcorn. My heart went out to him, wanting to protect him from whoever was threatening him. Life really had changed for both of us. I had been threatened too, after all, and still hadn't decided what to do about Billy. I couldn't talk to Matty about it either because he had too many things on his mind already.

After the meal we went out for dinner and drinks. We tried not to talk about anything too serious and mostly just used conversation to fill the silence. We were always the type of friends that didn't need to talk all the time. Sometimes sitting in silence was enough but I knew that silence would only lead him to think about the shadow hanging over his life.

The drinks followed one after the other and, gradually, we started to get sillier. I hadn't drunk like this in a long time, because it was frowned upon.

"You're being naughty aren't you?" Matty asked.

"Maybe a little but I think it's worth celebrating this reunion," I said. I noticed that our words were becoming slurred. The bar was quite noisy and crowded, but we stayed at our table and ignored the rest of the place.

"So what happened with this girl you mentioned?" I asked, unable to hide my curiosity any longer. I wanted to know the type of girl that Matty went for, even though it killed me to think of him sharing a romantic life with someone else. However, at the end of it all I just wanted him to be happy.

"Oh man, you really want to go there?" he asked, leaning back, rubbing his face.

"Might as well. I don't have any serious relationships to talk about and I'd love to know who finally took pity on you," I said jokingly. He shook his head and nudged my shoulder.

"Her name was Amanda. We met at the end of college. We'd been on the same course, but somehow hadn't run into each other until the last semester. Anyway, I guess I was filled with the spirit of letting go of my inhibitions so I asked her out, purely because I had nothing to lose. I mean, this girl was amazing, like, you remember Jenny Booth?"

"Sure," I said. Of course I remembered Jenny Booth. She was always the hottest girl at school. One of my claims to fame was that I had kissed her during a game of seven minutes in heaven when we were ten. Time hadn't been kind to her though.

"Well, Amanda was like the next level to that. Brains, beauty, she had everything. She'd light up a room whenever she entered it, and every time we were out people would stare at us, wondering how on earth someone like her ended up with someone like me."

"And how did that happen?"

"It's kinda funny really, you remember when we were kids and we always used to see the most stupendous looking women around, and we always imagined the kind of guys they would go for? Well, as it turns out, most people thought that, so she didn't actually get asked out often. Most people just assumed that she already had someone. I was one of the few to ask her out and she admired the initiative, so we had a date and I managed to be charming enough that she wanted to see me again, and it just went from there."

He took a sip of his drink and swirled the glass in his hand, watching the remnants of the liquid twist and tumble in the glass.

"It was easy with her, you know? It always felt like this was the way a relationship should be, and it made me wonder why I had always found it difficult with other girls," he added.

"So why did it end if it was so easy?"

"There was one problem. We both had different ideas of where we wanted to end up. She'd had everything planned out ever since she was a kid. Her parents had split up when she was little and she knew that she didn't want that. She didn't want to give her time to a relationship that wasn't going anywhere. Now, me, I just try to enjoy the ride, you know? Like, if something is good then keep going until it ain't good anymore. But she always had a plan for herself, and she didn't want to spend her time on anything that wasn't going where she wanted it to go."

"And where was that?"

"Where everybody seems to want to go. She wanted the whole deal, kids, marriage, two people melding together becoming something else entirely."

"And you didn't?"

"I don't know...at some points I thought I could be that person for her but then I thought why should I change? I'd only be doing all that for her, not because I really wanted to. I mean, I loved her, really and truly, but I felt like she was asking too much. We talked about it a lot, you know, and I told her that maybe over time I could change and I could start to want the same things she did, but she said that she didn't want to pin her hopes on someone changing their mind. She wanted to get her life started and I couldn't say anything to that. I could have lied, I suppose, and told her that I would change but then we'd be having the same conversation just six months down the line. It hurt like hell and there are moments when I wonder if I made the right decision. Like, if I had just taken the plunge would I have been happy? I might have been able to adjust, but I guess it wasn't fair to her to have to do that, so we parted ways. But damn I miss her."

As he spoke about Amanda I thought about my feelings for him. In some ways it was the same, because if I wanted anything to happen I would have to hope that he changed and adjusted to be more like me. Was that a fair thing of me to want? Was it right?

I didn't know.

We drowned our sorrows a little more. The more I drank the more I was tempted to tell him about Billy but since I hadn't decided what I was going to do about it, I thought I'd wait and see what happened. I hoped that it was just the product of the evening and that once I was in training, Billy would come to me and apologize, or just leave it.

We eventually staggered out of the bar, the smell of alcohol in a haze around us, the taste of it lingering at the backs of our throats and we walked down the street, just like we had done before. We leaned against each other and slowly left the main street behind us, slipping into the dark shadows of the town, where secrets were held.

"I don't know what I would have done in life without you," Matty said.

"What are you talking about?"

"Whenever I think about anything I keep coming back to this place and the only reason it holds any joy for me is because of you. You were the only reason I considered staying, you know. I've never really thought of this as my home. I wanted to get out as soon as possible, but I always hated the thought of leaving you, and I hate how I've acted. I should have made more of an effort to stay in touch. You were my best friend, my fucking best friend, and I let us drift apart."

"We both did Matty. We both made mistakes. We let life get in the way and we shouldn't have. We're better than that. Anyway, it doesn't matter. What matters is that you're here now and that we're here for each other when we need each other. You know that you can always count on me and I know that I can always count on you. Even if we're 80 and we haven't seen each other for 40 years you can be sure that if I need you I'll be coming to your care home to get your help."

"And you can be sure that I'll give it," Matty said, smiling, looking a little more relieved.

"And I don't care who you're getting involved with, I'll always have your back. I'll defend you and I'll protect you, because you're my best friend and I love you."

"I love you too, man," Matty said. Before I knew what I was doing I hugged him and as I moved forward our cheeks brushed together. I was filled with an urge. The heat of his body was enticing. The shadows in which we found ourselves were secret and the alcohol had lowered my inhibitions to such an extent that I had the bravery, the audacity, to kiss him.

My lips pressed against his and for one sweet moment his lips kissed back.

Then he pulled away and looked at me with an expression that broke my heart. He turned his head. I turned mine.

"I, um...I'm sorry," I said.

It was the last thing we said to each other that night.

Chapter 7

I felt like a prize fool when we returned to my apartment. I could tell that he was afraid to say anything. He probably wanted to forget that it ever happened, pretend that it was just a drunken mistake. All I wanted to do was crawl into a hole. Had I just damaged our relationship completely? Had I rendered years of friendship completely pointless? I wanted to talk to him, to say something that would clear up this mess, but the right words wouldn't come to mind. Before I could do anything else, I heard the door to his room shut and I had no recourse except to retreat to my own room and wallow in misery.

I couldn't believe what an idiot I had been. We had been close all day but in that one instant after our lips had touched there was a distance between us that was even worse than when we hadn't been talking. Matty needed me, and I had put my own stupid feelings before his. That wasn't what a friend did. Now, I had just added more confusion to his problems. I had to make it right, but at the same time I couldn't forget the lingering taste of his lips against mine, how soft his lips had felt, or the thrill that surged through my body over and over again whenever I thought about it.

Sleep did not come easily to me that night but it did come eventually. The last thing I remembered was feeling close to him, in finally having part of my fantasy coming true. I only wished that it could have been sustained and enjoyed, rather than tainted with shame.

When I awoke the following morning I was filled with anguish about how it would affect my friendship with Matty. I was almost afraid to step out of my room, and when I did so I found that his bedroom door was open and he was gone. I sank on the couch and went through my usual morning routine. There was no note, no message, no anything. His stuff was still there, and I wished that I could have waited for him, but I had to get to training. With a heavy heart, I left my apartment and went to training.

I arrived to the sound of much whooping and much delight at my previous performance. The only one who wasn't enthused was Billy but instead of glaring at me he wore a smug smile. I tried to ignore him, for I had much on my mind.

The coach got us in for a preliminary meeting regarding the next fixture.

"It's going to be a hard week and this is going to be a tough match. We're going to have to give it everything we have but I know that you can do it. I have faith in all of you and I'm going to keep faith in the same line up as just played. It was a tight game but I think with the confidence you gained from that victory you'll be able to sew up the game a little more quickly this time," he said.

I felt my heart quicken and for a moment I forgot about my strife with Matty. I smiled at the rest of the team, glad that I was going to be given a run of games in which to make my mark.

"Danny, you did a great job out there. I've been impressed with the way you've been keeping your head down and how you've been working to improve your game. You've earned this."

"Thanks coach," I said, swelling with pride, beaming at my teammates.

"Wait, coach, I'm fit enough now. I can play in the next game. I got checked out by the physio this morning and he says I'm ready. I can be back on the ice," Billy said.

Silence filled the room.

Before he had gotten injured it had been unthinkable to drop Billy. The man was a legend, an icon, and had given his entire career to this team. He was the most naturally gifted player on the team and everyone looked up to him with the utmost respect, including me, but to hear the plaintive tone in his voice was heartbreaking. Billy was getting old. He was in the twilight of his career and soon it would be time to hang up his skates. He wanted to get the most game time as possible and I was the one standing in his way.

"I'm sorry Billy," the coach said, looking pained. "Danny's been in good form. It's unfair to drop him now. Your chance will come again, I'm sure of that, just work on your rehabilitation and get back to match fitness."

Billy didn't seem satisfied with that. He scowled at me and leaned forward, tensing his biceps, a shadow falling across his face. I turned away from him, not wanting to imagine that he hated me when I had modeled my game on him.

The rest of training was awkward. I was already hating myself because of what happened with Matty and it took all of my willpower to focus on what was happening. After the coach's speech I didn't want to let him down and risk losing my place. Thankfully, I managed to make it through training without making any serious mistakes but as soon as I was off the ice I felt as though I was going to crash hard. The emotions inside me were turbulent and rumbling like an earthquake. All I wanted to do was get out of there as quickly as possible and get back to Matty, to talk about what happened last night.

But before I could leave Billy grabbed me, confronting me in a similar manner as he had done after the game. Everyone else was gone. I was alone. He had me pinned to the wall.

"I told you not to take what's rightfully mine," he snarled.

"I'm sorry Billy, but it's the coach's decision."

"Oh no, don't give me that crap," he said, the veins in his neck bulging. "This is on you. I bet you've just been waiting for this chance haven't you, waiting for the old man to get crocked so you can waltz in and take my place. Well I'm telling you that I'm not ready to lay down and die. You might all think I'm past it but I'm not. I'm still the main man on this team and you're going to have to wait a long time before I retire."

"That's not what we think at all Billy. Seriously. You've got it all wrong. I'm just playing like anyone would. You're my idol man, I love watching you play, I wish that I didn't play in your position but I'm not going to miss out on this chance. I have a career too, you know. But do what the coach said. Keep your head down. I'm sure there will come a point where I'll be rested and you'll be back out on the ice," I said, trying to be reasonable even though the man was fuming.

"Wait? I shouldn't have to wait. You know who I am. I'm a fucking star and if you think I'm going to wait, you've got another think coming."

By this point I was getting angry. All the respect I had for Billy was quickly evaporating. He was a legend of the team but he was acting like a petty kid. All my frustration about Matty started to simmer inside me, threatening to boil over and I began to struggle back against Billy. He was stronger than me but I was younger and I managed to break his grip. However, this only made him angrier.

"Why should I wait, hmm? I've been waiting for you to retire already. I've had my chance, I've taken it, that's how this works. That's how it worked for you when you got your start. You're the one with the problem here Billy, because you can't accept that your career is coming to an end."

"An end? Oh no, it's not mine that's coming to an end," Billy said. Instantly, his expression began to change. The anger faded from his face and I began to get worried. "How is your little friend?" he asked.

I furrowed my brow.

"What are you talking about?" I asked.

"The little friend that came to see you after the game. The little friend you spent some time with yesterday," he said. The color drained from my face. I gulped, my throat suddenly very dry.

"What about him? Have you hurt him?" I asked, my body bristling with tension.

"Oh no, I haven't hurt him at all, I've just been watching you Danny."

"What do you mean?"

"I'm very popular in this town you know. People are always happy to help me with anything I need. I told a few people to keep an eye on you and they saw how much fun you were having. One thing you're going to have to learn if you get more popular is that you have to be careful where you go, because there are always going to be eyes watching you. You'll have to develop a way of living where you can wear a mask in public and only show your true face when there's nobody around, like now," he said, his mouth twisting into a cruel grin as he looked at the empty hallway.

"What are you talking about?" I asked, still unsure what his point was, but the fear was strong in my mind.

"One of my associates followed you after the bar last night. It became clear quite quickly that the two of you were close. He saw everything."

"What do you mean everything?" I asked. Billy pulled out his cell phone and showed me a video recording of me and Matty hugging each other, then kissing. It wasn't a very clear recording, although there was no doubt that it was me. My eyes widened in horror. "That's not what it looks like."

"Oh no? I'm pretty sure it is," Billy said.

"We were just drunk and it's all shadow, nobody is going to believe that."

"But they are, you know they are, because people always want some little controversy. But it's not just this video Danny. I've been watching you closely for a long time. I know that you've just been waiting for the right opportunity before you take what's mine and I've noticed a few things. The way you look at the rest of the team in the showers for example; how you always blush when there are naked men around."

"No..."

"There's no use in denying it. I know what really makes you tick. And if you don't give me back my place I'm going to show it to the world, and your career is going to be in tatters. Hockey isn't ready for a gay player and all the people on this team will never trust you again. You career will be over before it's even started. I think we both know what's in your best interest Danny. I'm sure you'll make the right call," Billy said, sliding the cell back in his pocket. He chuckled to himself as he slithered off down the hallway. I leaned against the wall, feeling as though I had been sucker-punched.

If the truth got out I would be ruined. The team would never trust me again and what about Matty? It had already been humiliating enough for me to be rejected by him. I didn't need to have this plastered all over the locker room. I couldn't believe Billy would do something like this and whatever respect I had left for him was destroyed but I couldn't do anything about it either. If I went to the coach or anyone else I'd have to reveal my secret and I couldn't do that. The only thing I could do was to play badly and lose my place on the team but that just felt wrong.

I sank to the floor and put my head in my hands, hating that it had come to this. Hating that my life was such a mess.

Chapter 8

Eventually, I pulled myself off the floor and made my way home, even though it didn't seem like a refuge. My heart was in turmoil. I couldn't stop thinking about how everyone would look at me differently, how all the hard work I'd put in on the training ground would be for nothing. Matty, my best friend, the person who knew me best in the world had recoiled when he discovered that I was gay, how would my team mates react? As much I loved hockey I had to admit that the mentality in the locker room was still quite backwards and anything different than the norm was looked upon with scorn and mistrust. If they found out that I had been gay all this time, they wouldn't trust me, and that would wreck any chance I had of being a good player.

On top of that, I had the situation with Matty to deal with. I grit my teeth and clenched my fists, annoyed at how the situation had turned out. I was in danger of losing my best friend and my career in one fell swoop. It didn't seem right. It didn't seem fair. Why was I being singled out for this? Why was I having to suffer because of the gender I was attracted to?

I dreaded seeing Matty again because I didn't want to see the judgment in his eyes, knowing that it would only be a precursor to how the rest of the team were going to look at me. It felt as though everything was going up in flames and yet, it seemed as though this had been inevitable from the very beginning. At some point the truth was going to come out and it was going to come out because of a selfish man who couldn't accept that his time was coming to an end.

I walked into my apartment, almost afraid of what I would find there. I didn't know what thought terrified me most; Matty being there or him being gone. I understood if he needed space, but I didn't want him to leave completely. All the years of friendship had to mean something. I couldn't just let it slip into nothingness.

I opened the door and walked into darkness. The place was still, and it didn't seem like anyone was around. I went to the freezer and got out some ice cream, not caring about any diet or training regime. Right now I just needed to soothe the ache inside my chest and ice cream was always the way to go. I went out to the balcony and looked out upon the city. It seemed so easy from here, so simple. The world didn't have agendas or bruised egos or secrets, but the people in it, oh, they took so much and gave so little back.

When was the last time I was truly happy? I had been hiding myself for so long that it almost seemed I didn't exist, like I was a shadow of myself. The only time I was truly alive was on the ice, was it worth giving that up for the sake of not being outed?

Before I knew it, half the tub was gone and I groaned. The darkness behind me loomed and I wished that it would simply swallow me up whole. I had made many dumb decisions in my life and it pained me that if I hadn't kissed Matty none of this would be happening. Billy wouldn't have had any proof to blackmail me with and I wouldn't be coming back to my apartment with a feeling of dread sitting in the pit of my stomach.

As I looked out at the inky black sky, I noticed a piece of paper swirling in the wind. I felt like that piece of paper, as though nothing in my life was under my control. No choice seemed like the right one and I had nobody to turn to. I'd resigned myself to the fact that Matty had left. I couldn't blame him really, the shock of the kiss must have frightened him and he had enough going on in his life right now without me adding more stress to him. I had to figure out a way through this alone.

It was at that point, when I was feeling so miserable, that I heard a noise from behind me. The door opened and I could see the outline of Matty framed in darkness. I turned, wondering if I should greet him or not. He turned on the light and our eyes met.

"Why are you just standing in darkness?" he asked.

I shrugged. "It's calming."

Matty walked into the kitchen and grabbed a spoon, then joined me on the balcony. He took the tub from my hand and ate some ice cream, closing his eyes and moaning with delight as he did so. He inhaled deeply, and then stared out to the horizon, just as I had been doing. I remained silent, not sure what to say, or if there even was anything I could say that would make things better.

"How long have you been wanting to do that?" he asked. I furrowed my brow in surprise.

"What do you mean?"

"How long have you wanted to kiss me?"

"I don't know..." I said, my words faltering. Even I didn't believe them. He tossed a glance toward me and gave me a withering look.

"Come on Danny. I know you better than that. How long."

"Remember when you were Romeo? You had a way about you and when you kissed Juliet I couldn't help but imagine what it would be like to be standing there with you. It was a sudden thing really and I didn't even realize how powerful the feelings were at the time but it just seemed like such a natural thing."

"And all this time you've kept it quiet?"

I nodded, looking away from him, not sure what he expected me to say, so in the end I said the only thing I could.

"I'm sorry Matty. I didn't mean for that to happen last night. I just...we'd been drinking and spending the whole day together, you were going through a tough time. I guess I was just worried about you and wanted to be there for you, and I was swept up in the excitement of you being home. I didn't mean anything by it I just...I'm sorry. I wish I could take it back, I wish I could erase last night."

"Do you really?" he asked, and looked at me with those crystal blue eyes of his. I couldn't lie to him.

"No. I don't," I said, "not for the reasons you think anyway."

"For what reasons then?"

I leaned over the edge of the balcony and sighed. "It's not important. You have too many things going on in your life to worry about what's going on in mine. You don't need my troubles as well."

"Hey, come on, I thought you would have known me better than that. We may not have spoken for a while but that doesn't mean I've changed. What happened to what we said yesterday, about us always being there for each other? I meant what I said. If you've got problems then I want to hear them. Come on, let's go inside. I'll make us some hot chocolate."

We went inside and I perched myself on the couch as Matty made some hot chocolate and put the ice cream back in the freezer. He expressed dismay that I didn't have any marshmallows on hand, it was something that we would just have to cope with.

"So, you want to tell me what's up?" he asked, as he came over with two steaming mugs of thick, decadent liquid. I breathed in the cocoa aroma, something I hadn't smelled in a long time. Being an athlete was a rewarding career but there were a lot of sacrifices along the way.

While Matty had been making the drinks, I had been trying to figure out what to say. One thing that had taken me by surprise, was that Matty hadn't seemed to be shocked by the fact that I was gay, only that it had taken me so long to kiss him.

"Why aren't you more surprised?" I asked.

"Please," Matty said, giving me a withering look, "how long have we known each other? I knew you were gay probably before you knew it yourself."

"Why didn't you say anything?" I asked, shocked at his silence over all these years. Matty took a sip of his hot chocolate and winced. It was still a little too hot to drink comfortably.

"It wasn't my place," he shrugged, "I figured you'd tell me when you were ready and until you did I'd go along with the fiction. I just didn't know that you had feelings for me. That one you kept very close to your chest," he said.

I was encouraged by the fact he was talking somewhat normally to me but was still on edge about everything that happened.

"Well, thank you for that. Look...it's not like I'm in love with you, okay? It was just a teenage tthin and to be honest it's not like I've ever had a chance to get over you. I guess in my mind there's always been a sense of what if."

"What do you mean?"

I sighed again. This was the moment when I had to reveal myself to Matty and tell him what I had planned all those years ago.

"That night, when we went to Mabel's for the last time, I was going to tell you how I felt then. I don't know what I expected, if I expected anything but I thought maybe it would change things. But then we were hanging out and I didn't want to ruin anything. The friendship we shared was really special to me. Sometimes it hurt so much to know that you didn't feel the same way for me and I really don't expect you to. Kissing you was a selfish thing and I'm sorry."

I brought the mug to my lips. It had cooled now and I took a long gulp, feeling the warmth sink down through my throat to my stomach, spreading all over my body.

"I gotta say that I wasn't expecting this to happen when I returned home. It's a lot to take in but you don't have to apologize for it."

"I do. It was selfish and I should have shown greater control. If I had, I wouldn't be in this mess."

"I don't think that this entirely constitutes a mess," Matty said, laughing a little.

"I'm not talking about that, I'm talking about what happened today."

"What did happen?" he asked, so I told him all about Billy and what he threatened to do. Matty listened intently until I had finished.

"I don't mean to be insensitive here," he said, "but is it the worst thing in the world? People are a lot more accepting nowadays. I know it's a big deal for you, but if this guy wants to do this to you surely it's better to own it and hope that people will be open-minded."

"In a perfect world, I'd agree, but the sporting world still isn't ready for this. How many openly gay athletes can you name? The whole team functions on trust and if the truth comes out now they're never going to trust me again."

"Okay, but that's on them surely? If they want to be dicks about it then you're better off without them. I know it's not ideal but there are other teams out there."

"And which of those are going to want a player who has this controversy surrounding them? Which of them are going to want to bring in a player who is going to wreck morale? He's basically threatening to end my career before it's even begun."

"Well, he seems like a petty man and it's not right that he should be able to get away with this. There must be something you can do."

"There is. I can give him what he wants. I can play badly so that he gets his place back and gets to ride off into the sunset for another season and hope that when the time comes again, I get another chance. I'm younger than he is. I've been patient for this long, I think I can wait a little bit longer."

"No way," Matty said defiantly, "you're amazing on that ice and I know how long you've been dreaming about this. You've earned this chance and nobody has the right to take it away from you. You have to fight this man with whatever you have."

"How?"

"Well, first of all, you have to believe in yourself. You have to give yourself the chance to succeed. Danny, you're fucking amazing and I've never known you to take crap from anyone. This isn't any different. He's a bully and you need to stand up to him. Secondly, you need to own yourself. You shouldn't have to live in the shadows. You shouldn't be ashamed of who you are. You're an amazing man, the best friend a guy could ever have. You're funny, you're smart, you're kind, you're compassionate, you give your all in everything you do and you're a winner. You deserve to be out on the ice and if the outlook of these people is backward then you'll just have to be the one to move it forward. You've always been strong and I know that if you own this you will show everyone that nobody can bring you down."

His words were impassioned and they struck to the core of my heart. I was proud to be called his friend at that moment, and I blushed at the force of his words. He spoke about me with such pride and feeling that I genuinely felt special, although I was not sure if I had the conviction to carry through with his plan.

"It's not as easy as you think," I said.

"It never is," he replied. "But you have to start somewhere. You were never one to run from a challenge, not in the time that I knew you. What changed?"

"You left," I said. I was instantly surprised at how emotionally charged and instant my words were. Matty looked at me strangely.

"What do you mean?" he asked. I had to look inside myself for the answers, deep inside, where I was usually afraid to look. I took a long time to come up with the answer. Thankfully, Matty had enough presence of mind to let me think. I hadn't delved this deeply into myself for a long time but as soon as I looked, the answers presented themselves to me, as though they had been waiting there for me all along.

"I don't mean for it to sound like I'm blaming you, because that's not true, but when you went away I lost something. We were so close. I knew that I could rely on you for anything, so when you left I felt alone. The adjustment wasn't easy, you know. We went from hanging out every day, to not seeing each other at all, but that wasn't even the worst of it. It felt like I lost myself. I think it all hinged on that night. You're right when you say that I used to be the kind of guy that could take on anything, that could take the shots, but that night I didn't take the most important shot that mattered. I didn't tell you how I felt and from that moment on I lost some of my spark. I was more hesitant, began to doubt myself more, started to look back rather than forward. The ice soon became the only place I felt alive. That was the only place where I was able to succeed. I poured everything into being the best player I could but I've been living like a ghost. I think back to the time we've spent apart and I can't tell you anything of significance that has happened outside of the ice. I've been so afraid to take any risks that I've barely had any human contact and I know that I'm never going to have a friend as good as you again, so I haven't even tried. Though I guess that's more because I don't want to fall into the same situation again, where I'm suddenly feeling things for a friend that I shouldn't be feeling. So I closed off my feelings to the world and just lived alone."

"That's no way for a man to live," Matty said, his words heavy with sympathy.

"What else would you have me do? It was a mistake to hide my feelings but it was also a mistake not to tell you about them all those years ago. Sometimes, I just feel that life is too hard, that I'm not made for this world, that I'm not meant to be happy."

Matty leaned over and put his hand on my arm. He was so close to me that I could feel the heat from his body and smell the chocolate scent riding on his breath.

"Don't you ever say anything like that again. You deserve all the happiness you can get. It makes me so angry that this man thinks he can blackmail you because he's afraid of losing his place but I have my part to play as well. I'm sorry if you thought that I wasn't there to help you or that you couldn't confide in me. I never wanted to make you feel like you couldn't be yourself. Maybe I should have told you that I suspected something. If I had nudged you in that direction maybe it would have encouraged you to open up more. I don't know. All I know is that I'm sorry you feel that way and I wish that I could make you feel better but, really, I have to say that I know how you feel."

"You do?" I gasped. Matty nodded.

"That goodbye did feel like it had unfinished business. I missed you a lot. I don't know why I didn't call. I guess I figured we had to be grown ups about this thing and get on with our lives. This is the kinda thing that happens to everyone, you know? People drift in and out of our lives and nobody stays for very long."

"I never wanted us to be like that though."

"Me neither. That's my point. I don't feel like I've been complete without you. I feel stupid for having waited so long to come back here. Spending the day together yesterday was amazing. It's the best time I've had in so many years, which is weird when I had a serious relationship. You'd think that I should have more happy memories of that but, no, you're the most important person in my life. You're the one who makes me feel whole and complete. You make me the best version of myself and I don't want to lose that."

"But what about all your troubles?"

"I've been thinking about it. I've been thinking about a lot of things, really, and talking to you now makes it clear that we should both look at our lives and make sure that we are the best people we can be. Would we have have let each other get bullied at school? Hell no! So why are we letting it happen now?"

"Life isn't as easy as school Matty..." I began, but Matty had a passionate gleam in his eye, and his words were fired with inspiration.

"No, it's not, but the principles are the same. When we're young, we're always asked about what type of person we're going to be, what kind of man we're going to be when we grow up. We're grown up now. We get to decide that every day of our lives, in everything we do. I don't want to be the kind of man who gives up easily. I don't want to live in fear, especially when we know that we're in the right. I want us to be honest with ourselves and with everyone else. I want to be able to look at myself in the mirror and be proud of who I am and of the things I've done. I want you to be proud of me, as well. God, Danny, you don't know how confusing it's been without you in my life," he said.

"I can't Matty, this is my career on the line..."

"No, Danny, it's more than that. It's your entire life. That night, when you refused to take the shot with me, made you go into your shell, made you doubt yourself. If you give in to this guy, you're only going to be the same. You're never going to recover. Even if you go to another team, you're going to stay trapped within yourself. You need to own your shit and I need to own mine. I've decided that I'm going to go to the cops."

My eyes popped as he said this. He was speaking quickly, as he always did when he was in a fervor and his words blurred together.

"Wait, are you sure? I thought you said it was dangerous," I cautioned.

"It is, but it's also the right thing to do. I can't carry on like this. If I go any further I'm just going to be torn up by guilt and, eventually, it's going to catch up with me. If I continue working for them I'm going to be in trouble anyway. I'd rather be on the right side of the law."

"I don't want you to get hurt."

"I'm sure I won't. I've been thinking about it and I think I'm going to stick around here for the time being while this all gets sorted out. Maybe for the foreseeable future as well. I don't think life in the big city agrees with me. Besides, I've realized how much I've missed Mabel's pies," he said. We both laughed. I caught his eyes and saw that, really, he was talking about me and I had missed him so much too. However, I couldn't help but think about how much our dynamic would change now that my feelings for him were out in the open.

"But I really think you need to confront Billy, as well. Tell your team mates what's been going on. If they're worth anything they'll be there to support you and they'll all see Billy for what he really is. You can't live your life in fear, Danny. At some point, you're going to have to put your toes into the water."

"I'm not sure I know how or if I'm going to be able to get past the fear."

"You will be able to, because I'll be here every step of the way to help you," he said, and as he did so, his hand slid down my arm, resting against my own palm, our fingers entwined together. The touch of his flesh against mine brought with it so much delight, I gasped, but quickly composed myself. I couldn't let myself misinterpret his gestures of friendship, not when I had made such a huge mistake the previous night. I didn't want him to run away again.

But this time it was Matty who let his hand linger in mine, and who gazed at me with meaning. I was confused and thought my mind was playing havoc with me. I wondered if something had been slipped into my hot chocolate.

"Matty, about last night," I began, wanting to apologize to him again, to make sure there were no more misunderstandings. But Matty put his finger to my lips to keep me quiet.

"Danny, stop talking. You always get yourself into trouble when you talk. Let me talk for a moment. I'm the one that owes you an apology. I shouldn't have run away like I did. I guess I got freaked out."

"And for good reason, I bet you hated the feeling of another guy's lips on yours," I said.

"No," he laughed, "I freaked out because I wasn't expecting it and because it felt good. There's something I didn't tell you about the reasons my relationship ended. I gave serious thought to what I wanted out of life and part of the reason why I didn't want to commit myself to one woman is because I was never sure that I really wanted to end up with a woman. It always felt as though there was more to see and discover, more to experience. I never thought of myself as gay exactly, but I've always been a little curious, and when I was being rushed into making a decision about my future it felt as though I had to cross off a lot of possibilities and I wasn't ready to do that."

"What are you saying?" I asked, almost not daring to hope that I was hearing what I thought I was hearing.

"I'm saying, well, I guess I'm saying that..." Matty began, but instead of finishing off his sentence with words he ended it with a gesture. Leaning forward, he pressed his lips against mine far more firmly than I had done the previous night. This was no mere brush of the lips, this was a full on kiss and I felt it curl my toes. A hazy feeling filled my mind and

I could barely believe it when he pulled away, smiling at me. I thought I must have been in a dream.

Chapter 9

"What's going on?" I asked, looking around the apartment, worried that this was some kind of prank. Matty still had hold of my hand. With his other hand he ran his fingers through my hair. I tried to push away the feelings of arousal that swam through my body, not wanting to get my hopes up, sure that this had to be a trick somehow. Whenever anything seemed too good to be true it usually was and this was the best thing ever, something I had always wanted and it didn't seem like it could be real.

"What do you think?" Matty asked, leaning in for another kiss. I closed my eyes as his lips touched mine, then shook my head.

"What are you doing? This can't be real. This isn't you," I said.

Matty pressed his lips together and pinched the bridge of his nose. "This is me Danny. I know it might seem an abrupt change of mind since last night but this is what I want. Being back here with you has been amazing. I'd almost forgotten how easy it's been to just talk with you. It's effortless to enjoy my time with you and that's what I've been missing, that's what a relationship is about. I can't promise I'll be any good. I've never been with a man before but I want to. I want to be close with you, to feel you with me," he said, his voice dropping to a low, breathy tone.

I looked at him and he was as I had never seen him before. I could see that he meant every word he was saying. It seemed so strange to have him so close, saying all the things that I wanted to hear and yet I couldn't bring myself to fully believe him.

"What are you waiting for?" he asked, smiling.

"I don't know, I guess I've just been waiting for this moment for so long that I don't know how to process it. Are you sure you want to go through with this? Our friendship is never going to be the same afterwards."

"No, it's not, it's going to be better," Matty said. "We've been apart for so long that things have changed anyway. I want to explore these desires I have and there's nobody I'd rather explore them with than you," he said.

My heart jumped, leaping in my chest. I traced a line down the side of his face, down his chest, resting on his thigh. I looked into his deep eyes and lost myself in the ocean of blue. For so long I had fantasized about this moment and as I leaned in to pluck a kiss from his lips I knew that anything was possible.

Our breaths mingled, becoming one, and I leaned in, making the kiss firmer. I enjoyed the feeling of his lips against mine and how his arms started to curl around my body. Blood began to rush around my limbs as desire flowed like wine. It had been so long since I had been this close with a man, my mind and body went into overdrive. I was instantly erect, threatening to burst out of my pants. Matty noticed and chuckled, running his hand along my inner thigh, resting it against my crotch. I murmured with delight as I leaned back on the couch and enjoyed the pleasurable sensations that were running through my body.

Matty leaned over me, cupping my head with his other hand, kissing me deeply until our tongues were dancing. Although I still held my doubts about whether this was really happening or not, I was not about to let myself wake up from the dream, if indeed it was one.

I reached around to stroke Matty's back, feeling the broad shape of his body under mine. I played with his hair and nuzzled into him. Sharp tingles danced over my body and a prickling heat took hold. I started to get more aroused, the heat around us grew more intense, until suddenly we were clawing at each others' clothes, needing to get to the naked flesh underneath.

I pulled away his top, yanking it over his head, throwing it to the floor. He did the same with mine. We gazed in awe at our naked bodies, ran our hands along them, exploring each other, feeling the smooth textures and the hair, inhaling the manly scents. The masculine flavor that filled the air was decadent and indulgent. The simmering heat sparked and sizzled. My mind and body had been seized with the fervor of a supernova and I wanted so badly to be as close to him as possible. I enveloped him in my arms and tensed my muscles, which he seemed to enjoy. As we kissed, his hand fumbled with my jeans, deftly unclasping the belt, then he rummaged inside. I gasped as I felt him curl his fingers around my erection.

"Wow," he breathed into my ear as he maneuvered it out, standing tall and straight. His fingers ran up and down the shaft, caressing the bulging veins, his thumb stroked the smooth mushroom tip. Every inch of my body tensed under the force of the pleasure. He had barely touched me and I was already at breaking point, thanks to my years of solitude.

"Go slow," I moaned, and smiled as I felt the tight skin being pulled up and down, watching the delight dance upon his face as he learned how to pleasure me. I reached out with my long arms and was glad to see that he was equally excited as me. I clawed at his jeans and pushed him over so that I could strip him down and force him to be naked. I gazed in ardor at his manhood, my eyes looking at every inch of it. We were both big, both fine specimens of men, and we were both hungry for each other.

I fell on him then, kissing him passionately, ardently. Our hands battled with each other, digging into flesh, pain blurred with pleasure. Teeth nibbled at my flesh, I bit back. We were like two warriors, wrestling together in a long battle, linked together in a passionate display of strength and glory. The erotic nature of our battle surged through our bodies making us glow with heat, our bodies burning.

"You want to know what this is all about?" I asked, my words punctuating deep breaths and gasps. Matty nodded. I grinned as I changed our positions, guiding him to lay down, pulling his legs over my head. I rested my head against the arm rest, breathing in the musky scent of his sex. My mouth gaped open as I tilted my head up and took him in feeling the hardness fill my mouth. My hands ran across his back as he dipped his head down and took me inside him, wrapping his soft lips against my tight skin. We moaned and groaned, bobbing our heads in the same rhythm, taking every inch of each other, making the pleasure rise within us.

I took him as deep as possible. Saliva dripped down my chin. I could barely breath. The passion was suffocating, stifling, but I loved every minute of it. The only thing that felt better than sucking Matty off was him sucking me off. We had created a feedback loop of pleasure, which threatened to frazzle our minds and render us mute and limp.

But for the moment our bodies were entirely tense. We were joined in an endless circle, a symbol of infinity. Two bodies became one soul, two hearts became one love. All through our lives we had been linked together and now we were sharing the deepest levels of intimacy. I made love to his erection with my mouth, sucking and kissing it as though it was the most precious thing in the world. He did the same with mine. Sweat and sex mingled on our tongues. I could feel him swell and harden in my mouth until I thought I was going to burst.

Quickly, I pushed him off me and held him down on the sofa, leaning him over the arm. His mouth was raw where he had sucked so hard and he looked delirious. I towered over him, experienced and strong, ready to show him everything he had been missing out on. My biceps tensed. He ran his hands all over my body, feeling the hard, taut muscles, the body I had spent a lifetime honing to the peak of manliness. I cupped his head in my hands and felt the pulse in his neck. He gazed down at my manhood and opened his eyes wide.

"Are you sure it's gonna fit?" he asked.

"I'm sure," I said. I then dipped my fingers in his mouth until they were nice and wet. I delved into the shadowy parts of his body, searching for his sweetest spot, running the tips of my fingers around his most intimate area. A smile played on my lips as I watched him gasp and moan, loving that I was able to give him more intense pleasure than he had ever had before. Soon he was dripping wet and warm, ready for me. I spread his legs and held myself steady as I approached him, my breaths getting more intense with every moment that passed. Matty lay on his back, clamping his eyes shut as he braced himself for the impact of my erection.

I felt the inviting opening and pushed firmly, grunting as I entered him. I moved slowly, making sure that his body was comfortable with me. Matty burst out in sweet agony as his body had never experienced anything like this before. My head grew hazy and dazed as I thrust until I was wholly into him. There I stayed, holding myself still for a few moments, gazing down at the man I had loved for an eternity. No words I said could encapsulate the enormity of the feeling I felt for him, so I let my body speak for me. I took his hand and placed his palm against my heart so he could feel the thunder. I caressed his hair, then gradually I began to thrust. Softly at first, barely the hint of a movement, but soon I was seized by passion and couldn't resist the uncontrollable urges that overwhelmed me.

My hips thrust like pistons, driving into him with a deep desire. My face twisted in pure orgasmic delight, snarling in a primal manner, releasing all the frustration and desire that had been building up inside me since my teenage years. I was in him now and I was never going to leave.

I leaned down and kissed him passionately, our kisses were interrupted only by our satisfied, intense moans. I could feel his erection slapping against my tight abs as I thrust, our bodies rocking to a frantic rhythm. The intensity built inside. A tsunami started in the core of my body, building strength, gaining momentum, until it swept through me in one dramatic burst. My mind crackled, overcome by the heat, electric sensations rushing through my veins until I had completely lost all comprehension of the world.

There was nothing that mattered in that moment except myself and Matty. Time seemed to stand still as we lost ourselves to our lust and love. Our bond was strengthened. The years we spent apart had only led us back to each other and this was the culmination of all our agonies and woes.

I gripped onto him tightly, pressing myself as firmly against him as I could, screaming into his ear as the climax entered its final stages and erupted like a volcano into him, hot cum seeping into Matty. My body shuddered, rocked and trembled. The two of us convulsed and he clung to me dramatically as passion seized him as well and burst out of him in a pumping stream. I felt the warm drops lather my stomach, leaving us sticky and drenched in cum and sweat, a wrecked mess.

My chest heaving, I pulled myself out of him slowly, then collapsed on the sofa, drained and delirious.

"That was amazing," Matty groaned. I was too numb to speak, so merely nodded, and placed my hand on his thigh, squeezing it lightly. "Was it everything you've been waiting for?" he added. I looked at him and crawled over, leaning into him, stealing a soft kiss from his lips.

"I love you," I managed to say. A moment passed, then he repeated the words. They were music to my ears, and I knew that I could die a happy man.

Chapter 10

We moved into the bedroom shortly after that, after we had cleaned ourselves up. I sank into the comfortable, soft sheets, and welcomed Matty beside me. This bed had never seen another soul in it and I was so glad to welcome my best friend. We wrapped ourselves up and kissed each other softly. My mind was still reeling from everything that had happened.

"What are you thinking?" he asked.

"I don't know. I'm not sure I know what to think. I'm still coming to terms with it all."

Matty chuckled and twirled a couple of hairs upon my chest.

"This is a new beginning," he said.

"Are you sure this is what you want? I know this is all new for you. I don't want you to jump into anything you're not ready for," I said.

"I'm sure," Matty replied with conviction. "I know what I want, I know what I need. I haven't felt this happy or secure in a long time Danny. When I think about who I can trust in life, who means the most to me, there's only you. There's nobody else. I've been through so much, but when I think of the best times in my life I always think about spending time with you. I'm only half-alive without you, and I know you feel the same way."

"I do," I said, letting my fingers dance with his. "I'm still not sure what it means for the future though. What are we going to do about our problems?"

"We're going to be men," he said, propping himself up on one elbow, looking serious. "We're going to take our lives into our own hands. We're going to be the men we know we can be. I know what I need to do, and as soon as I'm able, I'm going to have a conversation with the police. The question is, are you going to do what you need to do?"

I leaned against the pillow and looked up at the ceiling. I blew out my cheeks and shook my head.

"I just don't know if I can. He's a legend. If I take him on I'm worried I'm just going to torpedo my career," I said, still afraid of what Billy could do to me.

"Danny. You're the only one who can make sure you get what you deserve. Is this how you want to live your life? I'm not going to force you to do anything you don't want to do, but you've spoken about trust, where's the trust that you're giving your team mates? Don't you think that they deserve some credit? They might not react as you think they will and I think they deserve to be given a chance. Yes, they might get freaked out at first like I did but they know you. They've played with you. They can see how hard you've worked and they might be able to look past their own prejudices. One person has to be the trailblazer and I think it might be you."

I grimaced. Matty continued, undeterred.

"I know this isn't the way you wanted it to go and it's not the way you wanted your career to pan out but what you've been doing hasn't been working so far. Hiding yourself hasn't led to happiness. Maybe it's time to try something different?"

I nodded along with him, knowing that he was making sense. If it was anyone else telling me this I probably would have told them to shut up and let me live my own life, but Matty had been there with me through everything. Deep down I knew he was right. All of my sorrows stemmed from that last night together when I had refused to reveal my feelings to Matty. Since then I had been afraid to own up to everything.

"You're right, I am tired of this," I said. "I'm tired of feeling like I don't fit in anywhere. I'm tired of having to lie to the people closest to me. I'm tired of pretending to be something I'm not."

"Then take your life back. Even if it all goes to shit you'll be able to hold your head high, and I'll be standing right there beside you."

Matty linked his fingers in with mine and squeezed. Just knowing that he was there to support me filled me with more confidence than I would otherwise have had.

"Okay, I'll do it," I said. He kissed me firmly.
I felt like a king.

Chapter 11

As I walked into the arena for training I was already sweating, and my heart thundered in my chest. Billy stared daggers at me. He was wearing his training gear, and was evidently ready to play. He didn't have to say anything to me for me to know what he was thinking. I knew he wanted me to fail.

I got on the ice, unsure when I was going to make my announcement. Matty was going to meet me afterwards at Mabel's. For now, I was on my own, but it didn't feel like that. I knew I had Matty's support, and that filled me with the confidence I needed.

Despite Billy's presence I didn't sacrifice any drive or commitment. Billy was getting more and more agitated as the session went on and it became clear that I wasn't going to act as he wanted.

"What are you doing?" he growled at one point as he passed me.

"I'm being a hockey player," I said.

Billy managed to hold his temper in for another hour, but then he let his frustration fly. He came crashing into me, his entire body weight sending me to the floor. My teeth clattered together and my bones were shaken. I picked myself up to see that everyone was staring at us, amazed at what Billy had just done.

"What the hell is this about?" coach asked.

"I'll tell you what this is about," Billy said, circling me on the ice but I wasn't going to give him a chance to say his piece. Coming out was something that I needed to do. It wasn't right for anyone else to decide when it was time to reveal my sexuality.

"No, I'll tell you what this is about," I said. All eyes turned to me. Billy looked shocked that I had interrupted him. "I have an announcement to make. It's something that might make you look at me differently, but I hope that you'll remember who I am and what I've given to this team."

"What you've given to this team?!" Billy cried scornfully. I glared at him, and that was enough to shut him up.

"I've been keeping a secret from you, and not just from you, but from the rest of the world. I've currently had someone threaten to expose me, and I thought I would talk to you all first before that happened, because this isn't something that I should be ashamed of. The thing is guys, I'm gay. I have been for a long time. I've been hiding it for obvious reasons but I can't any longer. I want you all to trust me completely, and I know that you can't do that if I'm keeping a secret from you. I want to be a part of this team for years to come but I'll understand if your opinion of me changes. I'm sorry for all of this, and I wish that I had a better way of telling you this news, but my hand has been somewhat forced." My eyes darted toward Billy, who looked chagrined.

Telling them the news had been easier than I'd thought once I'd started speaking, but my heart was in my mouth as my eyes fell to the floor, not wanting to look at the disappointment on their faces, or the horror and shock. I was already thinking about my next plans. Maybe I'd be lucky and find another club willing to take me on but I was sure that my time at my home town club was over.

Then something surprising happened. They started to applaud. I looked up, confused, to see them all giving me a round of applause. I was shocked at first and didn't understand what was happening. The only person not clapping was Billy, which was no surprised. Coach came over and put his hand on my shoulder.

"That's a brave thing you did son. It takes a lot of courage, especially when you've been holding a secret like this inside you for a long time. It speaks to your character and it's one of the reasons why I know you're going to have a successful, long career here. If anyone gives you any grief for this you just come straight to me. You have all our support."

I looked around to see the rest of the players nodding in support. I thanked the coach, then expressed my gratitude to the rest of my team mates. It felt as though a heavy burden had been lifted from me and I felt relieved. The rest of the team came around me and started teasing me, which was the best result I could have asked for. I felt at home with them, and as they all swarmed around me Billy stood alone. I knew then that I had taken his place in the team for good. His bitterness and ego had isolated him, and he'd lost everything that had made him special. He was nothing like the player that he used to be and that made me sad.

After training I made my way to Mabel's, unable to wipe the smile from my face. Matty was there waiting for me, and he too wore a smile. As soon as I sat down there was pie waiting for me. Matty kissed me too. It was a little strange at first to be so open about our new relationship, but I knew I'd quickly adapt.

"It's about time you two got it together. I've been rooting for you," Mabel said, winking as she delivered my pie. I looked quizzically at her, wondering how she had become so wise.

"How did things go?" Matty asked. I recounted what had happened and he clasped my shoulder, congratulating me. "How do you feel?"

"Amazing," I said, clearly relieved.

"Are you going to tell the coach that it was Billy?"

"I thought about it but I don't want to be that petty. Billy has his own problems, and he's going to suffer for them. All I can do is focus on myself."

"That's a healthy way to look at things. I'm glad to see that it worked out for the best. I think trusting people is the way to go. I can't wait to see you at your next game. I've a feeling it's going to be something special," he said.

"I hope so. What about you, any luck?" I asked. Matty had spoken to the cops.

"They welcomed my input. They're going to be sending someone to come and talk to me. They said they'll keep me safe after I told them my concerns. I'm still scared but I think it's going to be okay. I know that I've done the right thing."

"Yes, you did. We both did," I said, then took a look around the diner. "Who'd have thought that after all this time we'd end up back here."

"I know right. It's like we were always destined to be here. This is our home, this is what matters," he said, reaching out a hand across the table. I took it in mine and kissed it. After all this time I finally had everything I ever wanted and I knew that life was only going to get better. We'd both been through a lot in life, but after our years apart we were together once more, and I knew that we'd never be apart again. We'd gone from best friends to lovers and would stay that way for a long time.

I dug my fork into my pie and took a bite. The pie was sweet and life was sweeter.

*****

Don't miss out!

Visit the website below and you can sign up to receive emails whenever Van Cole publishes a new book. There's no charge and no obligation.

https://books2read.com/r/B-A-RTRV-VIQDC

BOOKS 2 READ

Connecting independent readers to independent writers.

Also by Van Cole

3 Man Huddle: MMM Best Friend Romance
His Alpha Wolf: Gay First Time Romance
A Dragon's Miracle: Gay Dragon MPREG Romance
Double-Teamed: MMM First Time Football Romance
His Football Star: Gay Second Chance Romance
Love In My Town: MM First Time Romance
Training A Hockey Star
Game Night
Double Shift
Take A Shot
Dear Professor
Getting Inked
Ninth Inning
Triple Threat
Seducing My Best Friend's Brother
My Protector
The Blueprint
Show Me The Way
End Zone
Matched To His Tiger
Love At First Puck
My Straight Boss
Falling For The Alpha
My Boss
On Thin Ice